TH.

JON JO. .NSON

Also available by Jon Johanson

the Ballad of Joshua Tree
Tonight The Sky Cries With Me
Trailer Park Tales
Not My First Rodeo
Postcards From the Road
Scenes From A Dream
Winter, Spring, Summer, Fall
Songwriter
Waiting in the Wings
Prisoners of Love
Weekend Break
Trick
The Colour Of Love
Tall Stories and Short Scripts
The Lodge
Jack in the Box

www.jonjohanson.com

CHAPTER ONE

"Men are such fools!"

"But you heard the news, Sophie, there's a mad murderer on the run from prison," Bryan said.

"Yes, from Hartsville, which is miles away really," replied Sophie, trying to calm her boyfriend.

"Not across country it's not,' replied Bryan.

"Don't tell me you're scared of the dark, Bryan?" Sophie laughed.

"I'm a city boy, you know that, we don't hear silence, you know nothing," Bryan replied. "I mean, I can hear the trees, it sounds as if they're singing in the breeze."

"Aren't they beautiful," Sophie asked him.

"We just get the Santa Ana's in LA, and there are lights everywhere, even on the beach. Can't we go back now?" he asked her.

"Let's just walk up the path a bit and then we'll go back, I promise, we've got the flashlight and the lights from our phones," replied Sophie.
Reluctantly Bryan agreed, knowing he didn't really have an option. His twenty-one year old fiancée, Sophie, was headstrong and independent, and he loved that about her – he just wished she would be a little more understanding sometimes, like now.

—

They'd agreed to get out of Nashville, where they shared an apartment, and spend a long weekend in the countryside after Thanksgiving, and get away from it all, 'find themselves'.

Sophie had found this cute little barn on Airbnb called The Lodge, that had been renovated into a quaint, rustic place to stay. There was limited electric, no running water, no Wi-Fi and hardly any signal for their phones. There was a large bed in the loft area, which had fairy lights on the very low ceiling. The loft bedroom area was accessed by a ladder.

When the couple arrived at the small farm The Lodge was on, they had been greeted by the owner, Cathy, who checked them in. She had also shown them the animals on the farm, including goats, chickens, ducks and a donkey named Belle, who Cathy said was guaranteed to wake them in the morning.

Sophie and Bryan had met at a honky-tonk bar on Broadway.
Bryan was in his last year at Vanderbilt University where he was studying to be a doctor. He came from a wealthy, Los Angeles family of doctors and lawyers but instead of going to a university in Southern California, Bryan had decided to break away from the family tradition and go to school in Music City, USA! It didn't hurt though that Vanderbilt was one of the most in demand medical schools in the world. A sizable donation from his father helped ensure Bryan a place but he was a natural doctor, with a keen interest in psychology and he planned to specialize in mental health.

Sophie meanwhile, two years younger, was a waitress. She dropped out of school early, got into a number of bad habits, including boys and drugs, but had crawled herself out of that world and the downward spiral it was going to lead her on and she was now attending school to gain her diploma and possibly train to become a nurse or at least a qualified in-home carer.

She was still a wild and free soul whereas Bryan was very much a young man who was responsible and reliable. It was these opposite characteristics that was an attraction for them.

"What was that?" Bryan asked sharply, pulling up and shining the flashlight around them in the dark.

"You, stepping on the small branch, stupid!" laughed Sophie. "Come on, let's just go up here and then we can go back to the lodge."

"Fine, but it's getting cold, and it's going to rain," Bryan told her.

"Great, rain on the tin roof, very Southern," Sophie told him. "Very romantic, puts me in the mood, you know?"

She kissed him quickly and ran away from him.

"Sophie, come back! Sophie, I can't see you, you're not funny!" Bryan shouted.

"Yes I am." Sophie replied from the darkness. "Come on!'

She jumped out behind him and startled him, grabbing him by the arm and pulling him with her.

"This way, come and see," she told him, leading him.

"I can't see anything in this darkness," Bryan retorted.

"No light pollution, isn't it beautiful?" Sophie said.

"I mean, look at those stars, Bryan, Mother Nature at her finest."

Bryan had to admit the stars were something special. It had been a clear night but clouds were slowly moving in.

"Come on," Sophie pleaded. "We're almost there."

"There, where's there?" Bryan asked her.
"Here, at that derelict house we saw when we drove in," Sophie replied.

"Are you mad, Soph? I'm not going in there, certainly not in the dark. Floors will be rotten for a start," Bryan said.

"We don't have to go in, I just wanted to get closer. I love old houses, they all have stories to tell," Sophie sighed.

"Well I for one can wait for daylight to hear this house's story, I mean look at it!"

Bryan shone the flashlight over the overgrown front garden and then at the house.

"JEEZ!" Bryan shouted, dropping the flashlight.

"Did you see that, Soph? Come on we've got to get out of here."

"See what?" Sophie asked, picking up the flashlight.

"The face, at the window," Bryan replied. "Come on, there's someone in there."

Sophie stayed where she was though, shining the flashlight at the house.

"Bryan, look, on the roof, is that what you saw?"

Bryan looked up and saw the light shining on a raccoon, who suddenly disappeared into the chimney of the house.
"How cute," squealed Sophie. "I always wanted a raccoon as a pet when I was a kid but my dad used to shoot them, pests he called them, I think they are so cute!"

Bryan was convinced or reassured.

"Bryan, did you see its face, the 'bandit mask' I used to call it, that's obviously what you saw," Sophie said.

—

"Maybe," Bryan replied. "Can we please go back to the lodge now though?"

"Yes, come on scaredy pants, let's get you back to safety! God, you're such a baby!"

Sophie laughed and ran back towards The Lodge, Bryan walking very quickly behind her.

*   *   *

CHAPTER TWO

James couldn't believe how easy it had actually been to escape.

Sentenced to life for the murder of two people following a home invasion that had gone wrong, James at twenty-five had nothing to lose by trying to escape. He had a long list of arrests that included burglary, fire arm offenses and assault and battery and he had been in and out of correctional facilities since he was thirteen years old.
Although he had meticulously planned everything the escape had gone so smoothly James thought that it would be a couple of hours hopefully before they had realized he'd gone.

It had been so simple too, straight out of a film he had seen years ago. No tunnels, no walls, and no one got hurt.

It was late afternoon, and was already getting dark. James was in the prison yard cleaning away the trash for it to be picked up. The truck arrived and parked and they started to throw the bags into the back.

James looked at the two prison guards, a male and a female, who were deep in conversation, laughing and obviously flirting with each other. James took his chance and literally jumped under the trash truck, reached up to the axle and held on tightly.

The truck started up and drove out of the prison yard, James clinging on, nearly letting go when the truck hit a pothole in the road but he just about managed to hold on.

They were soon in Hartsville and making sure there were no cars around or people, when the truck stopped at a red light he let go and dropped to the floor.

The truck pulled away without its passenger and James ran behind a gas station by the water tower. He sat down on the floor to catch his breath but he knew he had to move, and move fast. They'd soon be out looking for him, with the tracker dogs, so he had to put as much distance between them as possible.

He got up, looked around and walked quickly out of town. Once he reached the fields he got his bearings and started running, heading for the cover of the nearby woods.

*

CHAPTER THREE

"This is nice," Sophie said, lying next to Bryan on the floor in front of the fire.

When they got back to The Lodge, Sophie had made them a hot drink and they had played a game of chess, Sophie winning, again.

The radio was on, 92Q, a R&B station. At eight o'clock the news came on and the headline was the manhunt for the escaped murderer.

"I told you we shouldn't have been out," Bryan said, getting up and locking the door. "Who knows where this madman is, the police certainly don't by the sound of it."

"They'll catch him, they always do," Sophie replied, trying to calm her anxious boyfriend. "You should be used to this anyway, you're from LA! Daily occurrence there if I remember, shots in the night, helicopters overheard with their spotlights searching the streets and alleyways?"
"Well maybe in some parts, but not where I live," Bryan replied. "It's very safe there."

"Yeah, in the Hollywood Hills, but your family are wealthy, they have a lot of money, you have a lot of money from your grandparents. Most people don't have that kind of money, they're not left millions in trust funds, they live day to day, and in not so nice neighborhoods."

"I forgot," Bryan said, laughing. "You're only with me because of the money."

"I've always been honest, I told you that from day one!" Sophie laughed. "You called me your own personal gold digger!"

"Oh yes, you want to live in Palm Springs one day, don't you?" Bryan teased her.

"I do, and I will, I always get what I want," she told him, running her hands gently up his leg.

"Seriously though, Soph, doesn't it scare you? I know you're a country girl, born and bred right here in Tennessee, and guns, hunting and stuff, I've never met a woman who shoots until I came here, but it's like everyday life for you, normal, you can kill and skin a deer and cut it up, but Soph, this guy is a maniac, he killed two innocent old people. He didn't need to either, not really, it sounds as if he enjoyed it, got off on it even? He's sick."

"Yeah, he probably is, but we don't know his life story, do we? And anyway, as I said, he's far away from here if he's got any sense."

*

CHAPTER FOUR

James could hear the dogs far behind him in the darkness but he knew he had thrown them off his scent by getting into the water of a creek that led to the river.

The water was freezing cold through his boots but he had walked about a mile downstream, heading in the other direction that he knew the police and sheriffs would think he would head for.

A helicopter had been flying in the distance and he knew that they would be using heat imaging to try and find him but so far they hadn't actually come close enough to him.

Once out of the water James crossed a field. It was dark, no moon. His boots were heavy with the water but he had to keep moving.

At one point in the darkness he almost ran into a large deer, at first thinking it was a man, but the startled deer ran away, along with other that James could only hear, not see.

He came to a backroad and started to walk down it, getting his breath back and keeping to the hedge and staying away for the lights of the occasional houses he passed.
James was thirsty and hungry now but couldn't stop now.

He ran across a couple more fields, exhausted and tired and had to once again stop, the cold of the night affecting him badly.

He was almost crying with the exhaustion and the cold. He had tried to prepare for this, had studied other people on the run, who always seemed to stay in the same area, hiding in woods or caves, and James knew that that was a mistake, but he was so tired. He needed to find food, and water.

James sat for a moment under a tree, the ground damp, his head in his hands, almost defeated, when he looked up and saw a faint light through the trees. He got up slowly, and walked towards the light.

As he got closer he stopped and saw it was a small house.

Taking a deep breath, James started slowly and quietly walking in the dark towards The Lodge.

*

CHAPTER FIVE

"What was that?" Bryan asked, sitting up in bed, and banging his head on the low ceiling of the lost.

"A coyote, that's all, Bryan, they're in the woods around here," Sophie assured him. "You're making it cold, getting a draught under the covers, lay back down, you idiot."
Bryan did as he was told and lay down next to Sophie.

"A coyote? We have them in the hills you know, I should have recognized the howl," Bryan said. "It was probably the Tennessee, Southern accent of the howl that confused me!"

"Very funny, you like my accent, don't you?" Sophie asked.

"I love it," Bryan told her, reaching over to kiss her.

"What was that?" Sophie pushed him away,

"I heard it, too," Bryan said. "Sounded like footsteps on the porch?"

"Well go and see, you're the man," Sophie said.

"You're the one who can shoot," Bryan replied.

"It's probably that coyote looking for food," Sophie said. "It will soon run off if you make a noise and open the door. It'll be more scared of you than you are of it!"

"People always say that, like in movies and stuff, and it's never true," Bryan replied, reluctantly getting out of the warmth of the bed in his pajamas, and crawling to the ladder down to the main area of the Lodge.

Once downstairs, he looked back up at Sophie who was at the end of the bed but still under the warm covers.
"Go on then, get rid of it," she said. "Or we'll never get to sleep."

"Make a noise and open the door?" Bryan whispered.

"Yes! That's all."

"That's all, she says, in the middle of the night in the middle of nowhere, open the door!"

Bryan picked up a broom from behind the door, made himself as big as possible, made the loudest roar he could and opened the door.

*

CHAPTER SIX

James reached The Lodge and crept to a window.

He couldn't see anyone, but thought he could hear voices, but the trees had fooled him all night, talking to each other in the wind, sounding like a passionate conversation, branches hit out at each other.

James then saw the parked car at the side of The Lodge and knew there was someone inside.

He stepped up to the porch, accidently knocking his leg on one of the rocking chairs, making a noise. He stopped and heard movement inside. Staying still, and trying not to breath too loudly or make another sound, James waited.

The door opened.

*

CHAPTER SEVEN

Bryan came rushing out, shouting as loud as he could. James grabbed him and pushed him inside.

"Shut up!" James told him, closing the door behind him. "Stop shouting."

"Who the hell are you?" Bryan asked, but knew the answer.

He backed into the room away from James. Bryan saw a knife on the kitchen top and tried to grab it but James beat him to him, holding it outwards towards Bryan.

"Well this is perfect, don't you think?" James said, ignoring Bryan's question, and playing with the knife.

James looked up into the loft area.

"Hello up there, you should come down, and join the party. I can see you, you know"

Sophie got out of bed, wrapped a blanket around herself, and climbed down the ladder.

"Nice view, nice view," James said, acknowledging the fact that Sophie only had a t shirt on.

"What do you want?" Bryan asked James.

"Well to start, a drink, some of that pizza too," James replied, indicating a pizza box on top of the desk. "If there's any left that is."

"Just take the food, and drink or whatever, and just go," Bryan said.

"Oh, don't be so unhospitable, it's cold out there," James said, grabbing a slice of pizza, and hungrily eating it. "Excuse my manners, talking with my mouth full and all that, but I haven't eaten in hours. Come on, let's sit down shall we? You've got that warm fire there."

James pushed them onto one of the sofas by the fire, and sat next to Sophie.

"This is so cozy, isn't it? James asked. "After I finish eating, maybe we can get to know each other better, you know what I mean?" as he placed his hand menacingly on Sophie's bare knee.

Bryan got up to stop James.

"Sit boy, sit down," James told him. "In fact, sit over there on the other sofa. Now!"

Bryan looked at Sophie but she wouldn't look at him.

James moved his hand further up Sophie's bare leg and Bryan lunged at him, but James was expecting it.

It was almost like a game to him.

He hit Bryan hard, knocking him out.

James picked Bryan up and threw him down onto the other sofa, and then turned his attention to Sophie.

*

CHAPTER EIGHT

Bryan came too and opened his eyes slowly, hoping he'd been having a nightmare.

The nightmare though got worse as Bryan looked across the small room to see James on top of Sophie.

Bryan tried to get up but staggered back down.

"Oh, he's back with us," James said, getting off Sophie. "You missed all the action, you know, the fun."

"You sick bastard!" Bryan said. "Soph, Sophie, are you okay?"

Sophie didn't reply.

"Look at me!' Bryan shouted.

"She's fine, you know, and so am I, now," James taunted. "It's been what, a year or so since I've even touched a woman, and man, she's one hell of a woman, don't you agree?"

"Go to hell," Bryan said.

"Oh I probably will, you know, but hey, you still want her, now? After she's been tainted?" James mocked.

Bryan again got up, this time managing to get to

James and grab him but he was still weak and James easily subdued him.

"Kill him," James suddenly said to Sophie.

"What?" Sophie whispered.

"Kill him, Sophie," James repeated.

Bryan looked at Sophie and the look on her face at first puzzled him until the truth dawned on him.

"Sophie? Soph, you know this guy?" Bryan asked her.

Sophie didn't reply.

"Oh yes, Bryan," James said. "She knows me, I know her, and you know her, and it's like a family get together, still in time for Thanksgiving, except you're not family, are you? Your family is a long way away, right? In California. Your very rich family, I hear. Kill him, Sophie, so I can get out of here."

"So what, this was all planned, Sophie, you and him?" Bryan asked, incredulously. "Why?"

"A million dollars, Bryan," Sophie quietly answered him.

Sophie took out a gun from under the sofa and coldly and calculatingly shot Bryan in the chest.

He staggered back and just looked at Sophie.

"The life insurance policy we took out on each other, Bryan, when we got engaged, remember?" Sophie asked him. "Me, sole beneficiary. Two million dollars."

James got up and checked Bryan's pulse.

"He's gone, wow girl, great shot, I forgot," James told her.

James went to her and they fell on to the sofa again, this time Sophie on top of James.

*

CHAPTER NINE

"There's a sign there, 'No Smoking'," Sophie told James, pointing to the wall.

"You know me, Sophie, rules are meant to be broken," James replied. "So what's the plan now, you going to drive me out of here, I'll get in the trunk?"

"I think we should wait until light," Sophie replied.

"It will be better then, more traffic on the roads, all those trucks use this highway, Bootlegger's Highway it's called."

She had wiped the gun she had used to kill Bryan, clean and gave it to James.

"You might need this, you've got to get to Mexico, remember?" Sophie told him. "Now let's try and get some sleep, it's been a long day, a longer night, and we've got an even longer day tomorrow."

*

CHAPTER TEN

Neither of them got much sleep, both restless, waking up throughout the night.

It was Sophie who got up first, after Belle, the donkey on the farm, brayed loudly which was then followed by a rooster crowing.

Sophie climbed down the ladder and looked at the clock. It was six a.m. and light outside.

She went to the front window and peered outside, moving away from the blind quickly. She had seen two deputy sheriffs getting into position behind some trees. They both had rifles and she was sure there were others. She guessed that the dogs had followed James' trail to The Lodge.

Taking a deep breath, she quickly got dressed and then quietly woke James.

"We need to go, there's someone outside I think," Sophie told him.

"Really, okay, do we go together or just me?" James asked her.

"Together, Bonnie and Clyde," she replied.

They got a bag together and stood at the door.

"It might have just been a neighbor, trying to catch me in the shower outside?" Sophie joked. "Best be careful though."

"Sure thing, babe," James replied. "Let's do this, we'll run to the car and get out. Ready?"

"Ready!" Sophie told him.

With that, James opened the door and ran, only to be hit by a hail of bullets.

Sophie ran to the sofas and quickly put a rope around her hands.

"Help, help us!" she cried.

Sheriff deputies ran inside and secured the room.

"Thank God you're here," Sophie cried. "He killed my boyfriend, raped me and was going to kill me when you showed up. He heard you and didn't have time to kill me, just made a run for it.

"Well you're safe now, miss," a deputy told her.

"Let's undo that rope, get you a blanket and get you out of here."

*

CHAPTER ELEVEN

Two months after the murders at The Lodge back in Tennessee, on the top floor of a tall building in Century City in Los Angeles, Sophie found herself sitting in the offices of one of the most prestigious law firms in the city.

Her scheme had worked perfectly, and had gone exactly to plan, no one had even suspected her.

James had managed to escape as planned and make his way to The Lodge, which Sophie had found and booked as part of the plan.

She had provided a rape kit, which proved positive with James' DNA. The gun that had killed Bryan was found on James and only his fingerprints were on it, so that explained Bryan's murder.

"There you go, Sophie, a cashier's check for two million dollars. That's a lot of money," the Los Angeles based attorney who had handled Bryan's will, told her.

"Yes, it is," Sophie agreed.

"I have to tell you, Sophie,' the attorney continued.

"The insurance company were hesitant about paying out. They had an investigator look into the claim, and it appeared you might have known this James before, after all. It seems on his old Myspace profile, remember Myspace? Well apparently there was a photograph of him and someone who looks just like you. They couldn't confirm it was you though, the picture was too blurry, so they had no choice but to pay out."

"It wasn't me," Sophie said.

"Oh well. What are your plans?" the attorney asked.

"I'd like to start something in Bryan's name, his memory," she told the lawyer. "I plan on moving to Palm Springs, we were going to move there together one day. I have a few ideas."

Sophie walked out of the office, got in an Uber and drove back to the airport. She caught a flight to Palm Springs, where she had already found a small house she was going to buy.

On the flight there she thought again how simple it had all been. Both James and Bryan had believed her, men believe what they want to believe, every time.

Both of them really thought she was going to live the rest of her life with one of them? Was never going to happen.

She looked out of the window as her plane descended ready to land. Below her was the desert oasis of Palm Springs where her future was waiting for her.

Sophie had more than enough money to buy the house and to live in a very comfortable manner, and if she did ever run out of money, she was sure Palm Springs was full of lonely and gullible millionaires.

"Maybe a nice rich lawyer next time, an old one!" Sophie thought to herself.

"Men are such fools!"

*

Printed in Poland
by Amazon Fulfillment
Poland Sp. z o.o., Wrocław